P9-DVN-617

How a Shirt Grew in the Field

Clarion Books
a Houghton Mifflin Company imprint
215 Park Avenue South, New York, NY 10003

Printed in Hong Kong.

Library of Congress Cataloging-in-Publication Data

Rudolph, Marguerita.
How a shirt grew in the field / K. Ushinsky ; adapted from the Russian by Marguerita Rudolph ; illustrated by Erika Weihs.
p. cm.
Newly illustrated edition of 1967 publication.
Summary: Vasya, a little Russian boy, watches and waits through the seasons for the flax to grow that will be spun and woven into material for his new shirt.
ISBN 0-395-59761-7
[1. Soviet Union—Fiction.] I. Weihs, Erika, ill. II. Ushinskiĭ, K.D. (Konstantin Dmitrievich), 1824–1870 Kak rubashka v pole vyrosla. III. Title.
PZ7.R88Ho 1992 91-17838
[E]—dc20 CIP
AC

IMS 10 9 8 7 6 5 4 3 2 1

Konstantin Ushinsky

How a Shirt Grew in the Field

ADAPTED FROM THE RUSSIAN BY

Marguerita Rudolph

ILLUSTRATED BY

Erika Weihs

Clarion Books
NEW YORK

One day, Vasya saw his father throw handfuls of shiny seeds over the field.

"What are you doing, Daddy?" he asked.

"I am sowing flax seeds, so that shirts will grow for you and baby Anya."

This puzzled Vasya. He had never seen shirts growing in the field.

After a few days, Vasya went to the field to see if the shirts were ready. But all he could see was silky green grass where the seeds had been sown.

"It would be nice if I could have a shirt like that," thought Vasya, but what he saw was only grass.

Vasya's mother and sisters were in the field this time. They were bending low and stepping carefully, as they weeded the flax.

"Vasya," they said, "you are going to have a very nice shirt."

"Am I?" asked Vasya.

A few weeks went by, and still there was no new shirt. When Vasya came to the field, he saw that the silky grass had grown taller, and small, light-blue blossoms had come out.

"They are the color of baby Anya's eyes," thought Vasya. "But I have never seen anyone wearing a shirt like that."

More days passed, and Vasya wanted to see whether the blue blossoms were still there. But not a single blossom was left! The flax had now grown much taller, and some of the plants had little green heads where the blossoms used to be. The rest of the flax had dried-up brownish heads and looked very stiff.

"Something is wrong," thought Vasya.

His mother and sisters were pulling the flax out by the roots. They were tying it into sheaves and standing the sheaves up in the field.

Vasya shook his head sadly. "Now there will be no shirt."

After a few weeks, Vasya began to wonder what had happened to all the dry flax that was left in the field, so he went down to find out.

What a strange sight! His sisters were knocking off the little flax heads with paddles and pulling the flax into the nearby river.

"They must be drowning it because it's no good," thought Vasya. And, sure enough, they put large stones on the flax, so it couldn't float to the top.

"No shirt, and no flax." Vasya didn't say anything, but his sisters noticed how sad he looked.

"Cheer up, Vasya!" they told him. "Soon you are going to have a very nice new shirt."

"Am I?" Vasya was still puzzled.

In a few more weeks, the flax was dragged out of the river and left to dry again. Then Vasya's father hauled the dry flax in the wagon to the place where it would be threshed. Here Vasya watched his mother and sisters beat the rough, brittle flax with boards.

"I'm glad it's still good," thought Vasya. "Maybe something can be made of it."

The next day, Vasya saw his father haul the limp flax into the yard. Here it was shaken hard and beaten again with a special swinging tool called a swingle. The flax was beaten so hard that sparks flew in all directions.

"Oh, the poor flax," thought Vasya. "There'll be nothing left of it after all this beating."

The following day, Vasya's mother was busier than ever. She had brought the sturdy flax into the house, and was combing it with a big iron comb. She scratched it and pulled out the snarls and combed the flax until it was soft and smooth. Vasya thought the flax looked like baby Anya's hair. But it didn't look like a shirt!

"This will make a lovely little shirt for you, Vasya," said his mother.

"It will?" Vasya wondered what would happen next.

Winter came, and with it the long evenings for working indoors. Vasya's sisters tied the smooth, combed flax to spinning boards and began spinning thread from it.

Vasya watched them spin and listened to their singing. The thread was twisting and winding, and seemed endlessly long and strong.

Vasya's mother now set up a big loom in the corner of the room. With the thread, she pulled a base on the loom. Then, using shuttles full of thread, she began to weave.

She spent most of her time now in the seat of the loom. The shuttle ran quickly back and forth, back and forth, between the base threads, and Vasya could see plainly how cloth was being woven from thread—the same thin thread that was made not long ago from the combed, smooth flax.

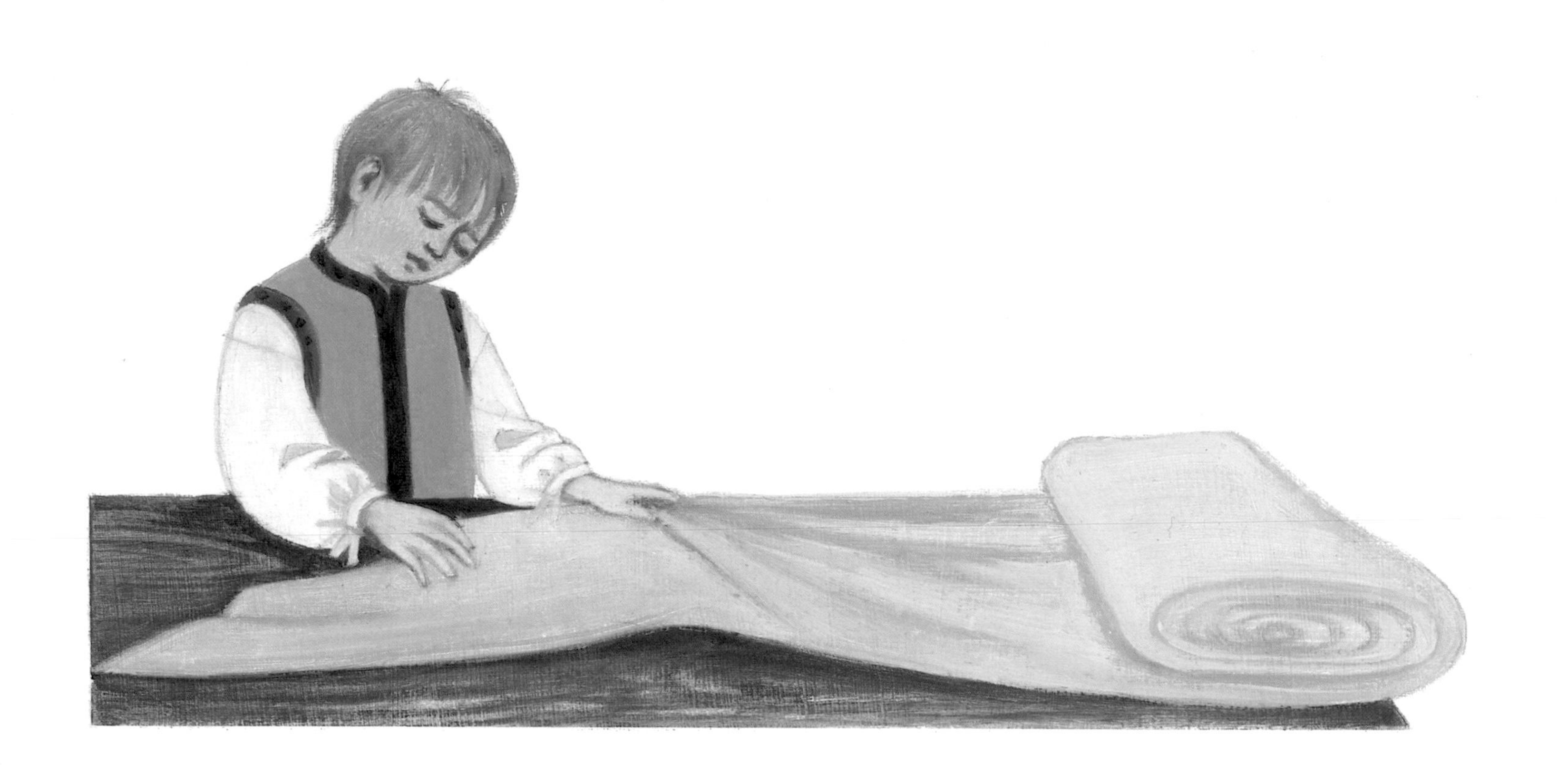

Yes, this was cloth—almost like shirt cloth! But it looked gray, and it was stiff and scratchy. Vasya didn't like the cloth very much, and he wondered what his mother was going to do with so much of it.

While it was still winter and deep snow lay on the ground, Vasya's mother carried all the rough gray cloth outdoors. She spread it on the white snow and let it freeze there.

"Why?" Vasya wanted to know.

"To soften and whiten it," his mother explained.

Spring came, and still there was no new shirt for Vasya. But something curious was happening to the cloth.

Vasya's mother and sisters dipped the cloth in the river and spread it out on the new grass to dry in the bright sunshine. "We'll have to bleach it more," his mother said, as she sprinkled the cloth with water. She sprinkled it again and again, and soon the cloth began to change. It was getting whiter every day!

Later, in the summer, the cloth was again soaked in the river and hung on the fence to dry and whiten in the hot sun. Baby Anya was big enough to walk around, and she pulled the cloth over her head. When Vasya ran over to pick up the cloth, he noticed that it felt smooth like a shirt. Would his mother make him a shirt from it, he wondered? He was about to ask her, but she gathered up the cloth in a heap, folded it into a large bundle, and put it away somewhere in the house. Vasya didn't know why.

One day early in the fall, Vasya's mother took the large shears and cut out a piece of the new cloth. She spread it on the table and went on cutting. She said she was making a shirt, but Vasya wasn't sure about that. He did not see how it would fit him.

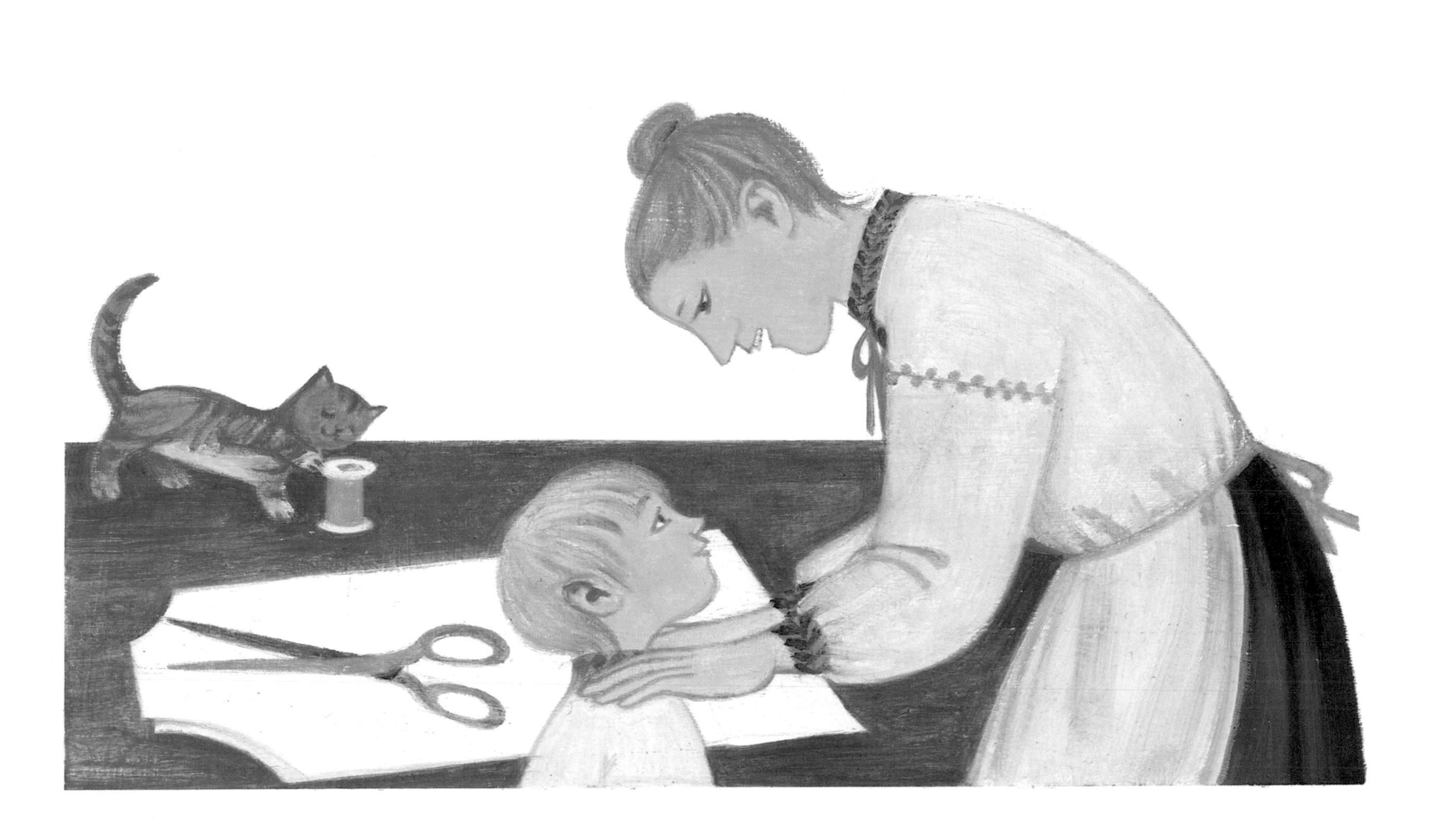

"It's so big, and it doesn't have sleeves," he complained.

His mother laughed and said, "You'll have a lovely shirt, Vasya!"

"When? Tell me!"

"Soon, soon!" answered Vasya's mother, and she gave the cut cloth to his sisters.

Late every evening for a whole week the sisters sewed and embroidered, but Vasya was already asleep and did not see them. Then one evening, as he was going off to bed, Vasya noticed his sisters sewing.

"What are you making?" he asked.

"A shirt for you," said one sister.

"And a shirt for Anya," said another sister.

"Really?" He couldn't believe their words!

Vasya felt so excited that he awoke in the night and imagined he saw a shirt.

When Vasya got up in the morning, it was light enough to see. There, lying on his bed, was a shirt! This time Vasya didn't believe his eyes. The beautiful shirt had an embroidered collar and cuffs, and it was exactly his size!

It didn't look like the green grass or the blue blossoms.

It didn't feel like the rough flax, and it wasn't a piece of cloth anymore.

It was a real shirt!

Vasya pulled his new shirt over his head, wiggled his arms through the sleeves, and tied the string on the embroidered collar.

Now he knew how his shirt had grown in the field, and he was the happiest boy in his whole village.

A Note

People have been turning flax plants into linen cloth for thousands of years. Russia and the Ukraine, the setting for this story, produced much of the world's flax fiber as early as the seventeenth century.

Flax (*Linum usitatissimum*) grows three to four feet high. Its five-petaled flowers are generally blue, though they may be white or pink. It grows rapidly and is harvested when the stems have turned yellow.

The stalks are soaked in water to dissolve the gummy material that holds the fibers together. After drying, they are beaten and scraped to remove the bark. The fibers can then be spun (twisted into yarn) and woven into cloth. The natural color of linen is yellowish or grayish, but the cloth can be bleached white in the sun.

When this story first appeared, more than a hundred years ago, all these processes were done by hand. Today they are done by machine, and Russia and the Ukraine still grow much of the world's flax.

Konstantin Ushinsky (1824–1870) was a Russian educator and writer for children. *How a Shirt Grew in the Field*, his best-known work, is considered a classic.